D0168483

SUPERCHARGED INFIELD

SUPERCHARGED INFIELD

MATT CHRISTOPHER

Illustrated by
JULIE DOWNING

Little, Brown and Company
Boston • New York • Toronto • London

Library of Congress Cataloging in Publication Data

Christopher, Matt.
  Supercharged infield.
  Summary: Penny Farrell, captain and third baseman of
the Hawks softball team, tries to uncover the reason for
the strange behavior of two teammates who have also sud-
denly turned into super athletes.
  1. Children's stories, American. [1. Softball —
Fiction. 2. Computers — Fiction. 3. Mystery and detec-
tive stories] I. Downing, Julie, ill. II. Title.
PZ7.C458Sup 1985   [Fic]   85-95
  ISBN 0-316-13983-1 (CL)
  ISBN 0-316-14277-8 (PB)

HC: 10 9 8 7 6 5
PB: 10 9 8 7 6 5 4 3 2

MV

*Published simultaneously in Canada
by Little, Brown & Company (Canada) Limited*

PRINTED IN THE UNITED STATES OF AMERICA

to Erin, Shannon, Kelly, Pat, and Mike

SUPERCHARGED INFIELD

ONE

FIRST IT WAS SHARI. Now it was Karen.

Who was going to be next?

Something very strange had happened to those girls, and Penny Farrell, captain of the Hawks softball team, wondered if anybody else was aware of it.

Shari Chung, the plump, dark-eyed catcher for the Hawks, had *never* hit a ball into deep left field before, yet moments ago she had knocked it some twenty feet over the fence. It was her third consecutive hit, including the two from the previous game against the Gray Wings.

Now, with the score 4 to 3 in the Owls'

3

favor, and the Hawks batting in the top of the second inning, Karen Keech had just lambasted a pitch out between left field and left center field for a stand-up double, scoring Gloria Johnson, the team's right center fielder. The hit was Karen's second one in the game — her first was a single — and the crowd was cheering her like crazy.

But what was so strange about it, besides the girls' getting the hits, was their *attitude*. Shari had not seemed surprised or impressed at all by her long home run, and neither had Karen by her hits. They acted as if getting such hits was routine, no big deal.

There was something else, too. Something that Penny couldn't quite put her finger on.

Pausing in the on-deck circle before going to the plate to bat, Penny turned and looked at the slender girl with the round face and large black eyes standing behind her. Maybe she would know.

"Kim Soo, what's with Karen, anyway? Is she mad at somebody?"

Kim Soo Hong, her bright yellow uniform about a size too large for her, squinted at Penny from under the wide brim of her cap and shrugged.

"I don't think so," she said. "Why?"

Penny looked across the infield at the tall, statuesque Karen standing with one foot on the second-base sack, the other on the reddish ground, and shrugged, too. "I'm not sure. But there's something . . ."

"Get up there, Penny!" Coach Mike Parker's voice floated to her from the third-base coaching box. "Bring her in!"

Penny glanced at him, caught his wide smile, and hurried toward the plate. In her haste she stubbed her toe and almost went sprawling on her face, but she quickly regained her balance and went on to the plate, her cheeks turning a brick red. Surely every soul in that crowd of some three hundred must have seen her stumble. Knowing the crowd was watching her made her wish she were taller for her twelve years and had wavy hair instead of that dark, straight mop that hung down the sides of her oval face. But she knew she had lovely hazel eyes and long lashes. You can't have everything, she told herself.

Alice Higgins, the Owls' left-handed

pitcher, sailed one in underhand that missed the outside of the plate by inches.

"Ball!" boomed the umpire, standing tall behind the catcher with his cap reversed and his mask on.

Penny glanced across the diamond at Karen on second base, thinking that if Karen could do it, so could she. If her memory served her right, Karen's two hits were the first she had gotten since she had rapped out two singles in their game against the Comets last Friday.

The pitch came in again. Penny swung and drove a hot grounder down to short. The Owls shortstop caught it and snapped it to third to try to get Karen, who was running there as fast as she could. But the throw was wild, and Karen scored. Penny went on to second base.

Loud applause rose and echoed from the Hawks' rooters sitting in the small grandstand behind the backstop screen and the bleachers behind third base. Penny smiled weakly and doffed her cap. After all, the hit — even though the Owls shortstop had erred on it — had knocked in a run, making the score 5 to 3 in the Hawks' favor.

"Hit it out, Kim Soo!" Penny yelled at the girl following her at bat. "Blast it!"

Kim Soo didn't waste any time. She cracked a single through short and Penny scooted to third, holding up there as she saw Coach Parker raising his hands high into the air. "Hold it, Penny! Hold it!" he shouted.

Penny looked at him as he stood tall and broad-shouldered, his straight blond hair sticking out from beneath his Atlanta Braves baseball cap like wheat stalks. He had once had a tryout with the Braves but wasn't good enough to make the team. Wearing the cap, Penny figured, might help him remember those bygone days.

Sophie Kowalski walked, filling the bases. Now the chances really looked good for the Hawks to get their much needed insurance runs. But Jean Zacks struck out, ending the half-inning, and every Hawks' fan in the place let out a disappointed groan.

Penny got her glove and ran out to her position near the third-base sack, shooting a glance at the girl playing next to her, Karen Keech.

"Nice hit, Karen," Penny said, wondering what reply she would receive.

Karen glanced at her. "Thanks," she said, and looked away. Smileless. Cheerless. Anybody else would have been thrilled about the hit and shown it. But not Karen.

Maybe she doesn't feel well, Penny thought. I'll have to ask Jonny.

Jonny was Karen's tall, husky thirteen-year-old brother, who Penny wished would at least give some hint to show he was aware of her existence. Maybe asking him about Karen would break down the barrier between them.

Rose Ramirez led off the bottom of the second inning for the Owls with a long clout to center field. Kim Soo, playing left center, rushed over, got behind it, and made the catch easily.

Janet Potter, the Owls catcher, batted next and drove a sizzling grounder through the pitcher's box. It looked to Penny as if it were going for a hit — until she saw Karen sprinting after it, trapping it in the pocket of her glove, and then whipping it to first base for the putout.

Penny stared at Karen as the Hawks' fans gave the shortstop the loudest cheer she had ever received. In *any* game. I can't believe it, Penny thought. Karen's *never* played like that before in her life!

The ball was thrown around the infield, Penny catching it finally and tossing it to Mary Ann Dru, the pitcher. The Owls' next batter cracked out a single over second base, and the next flied out to Melanie in right field, ending the half-inning.

Penny waited for Karen so she could run off the field with her, but Karen sprinted on by, totally ignoring her.

"Karen!" Penny called, the word spilling impulsively from her lips.

Karen slowed down, turned, and looked at her. "Yes?"

Penny ran up beside her, her eyes meeting Karen's, holding on to them. Where was that smile? That cheerful look any player would show after making a terrific play?

"That was a fantastic catch," Penny said. She wanted to say more, but just couldn't think of anything else.

"Thank you," Karen said. Even then she didn't smile, but turned away and continued on to the dugout.

Weird, Penny thought, as she found a space in the dugout and sat down, too. That's the only way I can describe it. W-e-i-r-d, weird.

Mary Ann led off the top half of the third inning with a single between first and second, but died on first base as the next three batters flied out. Shari Chung's long clout *was* close to going over the fence, but it was too high and not deep enough, giving the Owls right center fielder plenty of time to get under it.

Shari and Karen, Penny reflected. They both have been playing much, *much* better softball than they have ever played before. What had they been doing? Practicing at night? Penny doubted it. They didn't practice any more than any of the other players.

Then what was it? *What had made them so good?*

The Owls went scoreless during their turn at bat. Then Gloria started off the top of the fourth with a single over first, bringing up the top of the batting order again, Karen.

"Sock it out, Karen!" a fan yelled from the stands behind the backstop screen, and Penny recognized Jonny's voice. She smiled as she saw him sitting there among his buddies, cheering for his sister.

The first pitch came in, and Karen *did*

sock it out. The ball sailed over the center-field fence for a whopping home run.

Penny hardly noticed the team leaping out of the dugout, pushing past her, and going to the plate to congratulate Karen. She was too stunned by the magnitude of that home run. Karen wasn't a very strong girl. Where had she gotten all that power?

"It's hard to believe, isn't it?" a low, drawling voice said beside her.

Penny turned and saw Harold Dempsey, the team's scorekeeper, smiling at her.

"It sure is," Penny answered, then snapped out of her confusion and went to offer Karen her congratulations, too.

TWO

KAREN'S TWO-RUN HOMER put the Hawks ahead of the Owls by three runs, 7 to 4. But the Owls rallied during their turn at bat and tied the score.

In spite of the Owls' rally, however, Penny was sure that other members of the Hawks team, especially Coach Parker, must have noticed how well Shari and Karen were shining at bat and in the infield. Shari was catching Mary Ann's pitches and returning them as if she'd been born behind the plate. And she had already knocked out a home run. Everyone could see that Karen was playing far above her normal ability, too. Those hits she had banged out were not accidental. They were solidly hit.

"If the rest of us played half as well as Shari and Karen, we should win this game. And, boy, do we need another win!" exclaimed Faye Marsh, swinging a bat in the on-deck circle.

Penny, standing at the side of the dugout, took her gaze away from the leadoff batter, Mary Ann, and looked at her red-haired friend. "The way Shari and Karen are playing, we might not have to play half as well," she said soberly.

"Right," Faye agreed. She stopped swinging her bat for a minute to rub her nose. "Remember the game against the Gray Wings? Shari got a homer and a couple of singles in that. Now she's already got a homer in this game. Where did she get all that energy, anyway?"

"Good question," answered Penny. "And she *was* hitting pretty lousy in the games before that, wasn't she?"

"Lousy is right," said Faye.

Penny sighed. "I don't know," she said, turning her attention back to Mary Ann. "She and Karen are doing something right, that's for sure."

The words had barely left her mouth, when Mary Ann swung at a high pitch and slammed it to shallow center field. Pauline Case ran in about a half a dozen steps, reached down, and caught it.

"Tough luck, Mary Ann," Penny cried. "Okay, Faye. Get a hit."

Faye did: a sharp double to deep left center field. Penny smiled, then watched as Melanie strode to the plate, carrying a bat across her right shoulder.

Short, blond, and just slightly chubby, Melanie stood in the batting box, took a called ball and a strike, then cracked a sharp grounder to deep short. The shortstop fielded it perfectly and winged it to first, but Melanie beat the throw by half a step.

"Way to go, Mel!" Penny yelled, leaping out of the dugout and clapping so hard her palms stung. It was Melanie's first hit of the game.

Then Shari came up, and Penny sat down and watched her, wondering what Shari would do now. The plump, dark-haired Chinese girl leaned into the first pitch and drilled it into deep left center field. Two runs scored, and Shari stood on second base for a double. Penny stared at her, wondering if there was some kind of hex mixed up in this. She didn't believe in that sort of thing, but there *was* something fishy going on with Shari and Karen. Of that she was sure.

Gloria smashed a hard grounder down to first base, which Josie Slade, the Owls first baseman, scooped up and dashed to first for the putout.

"Third! Third!" a cry rang out from the Owls dugout. But by the time Josie turned and brought her arm back to throw to third base, Shari was already there. Penny, standing in the dugout next to Harold, could hardly believe it.

"Did you see her run?" Penny exclaimed, her voice high-pitched with surprise. "Did you?"

"Like the wind. Right?"

Harold was smiling mysteriously at her.

"That's right. Like the wind," Penny echoed, and sat down, feeling as if she had made the run from second base to third herself.

"Two hits and a steal," Harold said, reading the statistics from the scorebook he was holding. "Not bad, right?"

"No, not bad at all," Penny agreed. "And

please stop saying 'right' all the time. Okay?" she added curtly.

Harold grinned, showing teeth with wide gaps between them. "Okay," he promised.

How and why he had become the team's scorekeeper Penny couldn't even guess, nor did she care. Having the same person keep score at every game was great, though, especially since he enjoyed it. Harold had been the team's official scorekeeper since their third game. He was short for his eleven years, stocky, and had thick, curly black hair that covered the tops of his ears. His nose, stuck in the middle of his round face, looked as if he had bumped it into something solid and it had never returned to its original shape. His eyes were dark and curious, as if everything he looked at interested him. And a lot of it did. His hobby was fooling around with the computer that was given to him by his father, a computer-and-science teacher at the Tall Oaks Junior High School. Why Harold preferred to spend his time keeping score at softball games instead of playing with that computer was a mystery to Penny.

She saw Karen walking to the plate and dismissed the thought of Harold from her mind. Karen stood there, waving the bat in a small circle over her right shoulder as she watched the Owls pitcher with a cool, intense gaze.

"Pick up a bat and get up there, Penny," Harold advised. "You're up next."

As if in a fog, Penny jumped out of the dugout, grabbed her favorite bat, and stepped into the on-deck circle. The first pitch to Karen was a high fast ball, and she let it go. The next was down by her knees and she swung at it.

The sound of bat connecting with ball was solid, and Penny held her breath as she saw the ball streaking out to deep center field as if it were shot out of a cannon. It's going to be another homer, she thought.

But the hit was too shallow, and the Owls right center fielder caught it over her head for the third out.

"Almost but not quite," Penny heard Harold say from the dugout.

Oh, please, shut up, will you? Penny wanted to shout at him as she dropped her bat and returned to the dugout for her glove. But "almost but not quite" *was* right, Penny thought. She was beginning to think Karen wasn't human anymore. Breathing a sigh,

Penny got her glove and ran out to her position at third.

The Owls picked up a run during their turn at bat and two more in the bottom of the sixth to go into the lead, 10 to 9. Penny had hoped that Shari, batting third in the top of the seventh inning with two outs, might spring again with a long clout that would tie up the game and give the Hawks another chance to win. But all Shari could do was crack out a single. Then Gloria grounded out, and the game went to the Owls.

"Shari, can I see you for a minute?" Penny called, running onto the infield to meet the girl as she came running in.

"Sorry. I have to get home," Shari answered.

"But —"

"Sorry," Shari repeated, and hurried to the dugout to pick up her catcher's mitt and mask.

THREE

PENNY LOOKED AROUND for Karen and saw her walking off the field with Jonny. He was looking at her and talking to her in that friendly, vibrant way of his. The sight of him made her forget even Karen for a moment. She knew she was too young to date, and Jonny was the first boy she had ever taken an interest in. The only trouble was, he hardly knew she existed.

Had he noticed the change in his sister? Penny wondered. How could he *not* have?

She heard footsteps behind her and turned around to see Shari rushing away from the dugout with her mitt.

"Shari! You okay?" Penny called to her.

"I'm fine!" Shari shot back over her shoulder.

Penny saw Harold and Coach Parker look up at her from the dugout, a curious look on their faces, and she quickly turned away, hoping they wouldn't ask her what had made her say that.

Just then Faye ran up to her, and Penny felt relieved. She took Faye's hand and propelled her away from the dugout and across the infield.

"Hey! What's the hurry?" Faye exclaimed, pulling her cap down firmly over her thick red hair.

"Just wanted to get away from those two before they start asking me questions," Penny answered. She bobbed her head toward Harold and Coach Parker.

"Questions? Why?"

They headed toward the left side of the backstop screen by the gate, Penny maintaining a rapid, one-step lead on Faye.

"Have you noticed anything different about Shari and Karen?" Penny asked, trying to keep her nervous excitement under control.

"Well, they certainly played much better softball in today's game than in any games before this," Faye observed.

"Yes, but I'm talking about something else," Penny said. "Something about their behavior. Particularly *after* they got their hits."

Faye paused and relaxed her grip on Penny's hand. Penny stopped and looked at her. "Penny, just what are you trying to say?"

"Well, think," said Penny seriously. "If you got a double, or a home run, and the crowd cheered for you like crazy, wouldn't you smile at them, or tip your cap at them? Wouldn't you do *something* to show your appreciation?"

"Yes. I think I would."

"I think you would, too. I think most kids would. But did Shari or Karen? No."

Faye's green eyes went wide, and her mouth parted in a tiny oval. "Hey! Now that you mention it, I did notice that! But —" She tipped her head down slightly and narrowed her eyes to slits. "I don't know what you're driving at, Penny. But I think you're making something out of nothing. Maybe Shari and Karen are having a hot streak and can't get over the shock themselves." She started running ahead of Penny. "Sorry, but I feel my stomach touching sides, and you know what that means! See ya later, alligator!"

Penny stood, watching Faye racing through the gate and down the sidewalk, locks of her red hair bobbing beneath the back of her softball cap. Penny frowned, thinking, Maybe Faye's right. Maybe I *am* making something out of nothing. But it sure is funny the way those two girls have suddenly started acting.

She continued through the gate and was on the sidewalk when she heard a familiar voice calling her name. "Hey, Penny! Wait a minute!"

She spun and saw Harold Dempsey running toward her, carrying his scorebook. Suddenly the scorebook gave her an idea, so she didn't mind waiting, even though her stomach was touching sides, too.

"Thanks, Penny!" Harold exclaimed breathlessly as he popped around the open gate and stopped beside her. "Man! I'm out of shape!"

Penny flashed a grin. "You need more exercise, Harold," she said amiably. "Just sitting in front of that computer won't do it, you know."

He smiled. "I know."

"May I look at that scorebook a minute?" she asked, reaching for it.

"Sure."

She turned to the second page, which showed the box scores of the Hawks' first game, glanced at Karen Keech's name at the top, and read off Karen's at-bat record silently. No hits.

Penny ran her forefinger down the lineup column to Shari Chung's name, read her statistics, and saw that Shari had gotten one hit. She turned to the next page and saw that Karen had not gotten a hit in that game either, and neither had Shari. Karen had broken her hitless streak in the third game — against the Comets last Friday — getting two singles. Shari had gotten three hits, including a triple.

"Checking on somebody's hitting record, Penny?" Harold asked, his deep voice more like an adult's than a kid's.

"Yes. But —" Penny cut herself off short. Why should she tell Harold her discovery, anyway? He wouldn't know what she was talking about.

"But what?" he asked.

"But nothing," she replied. She closed the scorebook and handed it back to him. "Thanks, Harold. You're a king . . . or a prince . . . or whatever. Well, I've got to get home and shower. See you at the next game. Okay?"

"Penny, wait!" Harold shouted after her as she started to run off. "I want to ask you something!"

She stopped, turned, and watched him walking hurriedly toward her. "Ask me what?"

He cleared his throat. "Will you go to a movie with me this Saturday afternoon? There's a good adventure —"

"A movie? With you? Are you —" Penny almost said "crazy" but caught herself in time. "Sorry, Harold," she went on, blushing slightly. "I . . . ah . . . I think I'm going to be busy Saturday afternoon. But, thanks, anyway. Okay? See you!"

She turned and sprinted away, grabbing her cap before the wind could blow it off. Imagine Harold asking *me* to go to a movie with him, she thought. What nerve! Now, if that were Jonny . . .

FOUR

SHORTLY AFTER SEVEN O'CLOCK
that evening, Penny telephoned Karen. She
couldn't get the thought of her strange behavior out of her mind, and figured that the
best way to get to the root of the matter was
to talk to her personally.

Mrs. Keech answered.

"This is Penny Farrell," said Penny. "Can
I talk to Karen, please?"

"Karen's in her room, Penny," Mrs. Keech
answered. She had a soft, low-pitched voice
that made her sound as if she were holding
the telephone too far away. "She doesn't feel
well."

"Oh. I'm sorry," said Penny.

"Nothing serious, I don't think," Mrs. Keech went on. "She played a pretty hard game this afternoon, Jonny said, and must be tired. Any message you want me to give her?"

"No. I just wanted to talk with her, that's all. Thank you."

"I'll tell her you called," Mrs. Keech said.

"No, that's okay," Penny said quickly. "You don't need to."

She hung up, feeling no different now than she had before she talked with Mrs. Keech. Except that even Mrs. Keech did not seem to suspect anything unnatural in Karen's behavior.

Karen ill? Perhaps, but it's not the kind of illness I've ever seen before, Penny thought. Nobody can be ill and play the kind of ball game that Karen had played. Or Shari, either, for that matter.

I wonder if I'll ever know the truth, Penny thought. Does Jonny know? Penny tried to imagine the conversation that might have taken place if he had answered the telephone instead of his mother. It might have fizzled like a damp fuse, she thought. *What can I do to make him notice me?*

She went into the living room and glanced

at the tall, oak-brown grandfather clock standing in the far corner. It was almost a quarter after seven.

Her mother and father were sitting in their favorite easy chairs, watching television. They glanced up at her, and Mrs. Farrell smiled. "I heard you ask about Karen, dear. Is she all right?"

Mrs. Farrell was a tall, slim woman with warm brown eyes, heavy eyebrows, and wavy black hair that Penny had so often wished she had inherited.

"She's in bed," Penny answered. "Played a hard game, her mother thinks."

"Well, didn't you?" said Mr. Farrell.

Penny glanced at her father, saw his hazel eyes twinkling, and shrugged. "Maybe she didn't feel well during the game," Penny replied, just to say something.

Mr. Farrell grinned, pushed back a strand of blond hair that had fallen over his face, and resumed watching TV.

"Okay if I ride my bike over to Faye's?" Penny asked, shooting her eyes from her mother to her father to show them that her question was impartial.

"Of course. Just watch out for traffic," her mother said warningly.

"And get home before dark," her father added.

Penny smiled at them. "Don't I always?" she said. She turned and darted out of the room to the back door.

Penny got her bike out of the two-car garage and rode down the street toward Faye's house. But when she reached the intersection of Teall and Meadow, she turned left. The Keeches lived in the fourth house on the right on Meadow Street, and maybe, just maybe, Jonny would be out there in the backyard, mowing the lawn or something.

Penny rode past the house, glancing over the hedgerow into the backyard, hoping . . . hoping . . .

Her heart skipped a beat as she saw Jonny. He *was* out there! Playing catch with someone!

"Hi, Jonny!" she cried, excitement in her voice.

He looked around at her and waved. Then Penny saw whom he was playing catch with. It was Karen!

Well! Penny thought, surprised. She certainly got well quickly!

Penny braked, pulled up to the curb, and got off the bike. "Hi, Karen!" she called.

Karen caught her brother's throw, glanced briefly at Penny, said hi, and returned the throw to Jonny. She showed no emotion whatever — neither pleasure nor displeasure at seeing Penny. Penny was more certain now than ever that something was wrong with Karen.

She stood balancing herself, one foot on a pedal, the other on the street, wanting desperately to go and talk with Karen. But Karen's impassive, cool attitude held her back. Penny thought that if Jonny would only invite her into their yard, her problem might easily be solved. But he didn't.

"Played a terrific game today, Karen," Penny said, breaking the awkward silence.

"Thank you."

The reply was soft, almost inaudible.

"We should've won the game," Penny added.

"I know."

Jonny caught the next pitch from Karen, folded the fingers of his glove firmly over the ball, and grinned across at his sister. "Well, I've had enough," he said. "How about you?"

"Yes." Karen turned and started to head for the house, and Jonny looked at Penny. "How you doing?"

Penny shrugged. "Okay." She couldn't think of anything else to say for a moment.

"Mom said you called and asked about Karen," Jonny went on in that pleasant, velvety voice of his. His straight blond hair was a little unruly in front, dangling over his forehead, and his nose seemed to be too small for his wide face. But his smile now overshadowed that minor oversight of nature's, and Penny smiled back.

"Well, she . . . she didn't seem to be saying much, and I just wondered if she was okay," Penny said, feeling uncomfortable and nervous.

"She *was* a little tired," said Jonny. "But she rested awhile and is fine now. Thanks for asking." He headed for the house. "Take care."

"You, too," said Penny. She watched him as he walked toward the back door, then she got on her bike and rode off. He knows there's something fishy about Karen, too, Penny thought. He knows as well as I do. Why doesn't he say something?

Penny found Faye and Mrs. Marsh trimming rosebushes in their backyard.

"Uh oh," Penny muttered, remaining on her bike as she watched mother and daughter from the narrow sidewalk leading to their back door. "I guess I should have telephoned."

Faye and her mother glanced up simultaneously. Both smiled, surprised to see her. "Oh, hi!" said Faye. "Telephoned? Why?"

Penny grinned. "I never *dreamed* you'd be working."

"You call this work?" Faye cried. "I'm cutting in on Mom's hobby. And you know what? It's fun!"

Mrs. Marsh straightened up, moved her shoulders back and forth, and stroked away some of her straight black hair, which had fallen over her slender, cheerful face.

"If it's so much fun, how come I've trimmed three bushes so far, and you only one?" Mrs. Marsh asked, and smiled. "Go on. Get your bike and go riding with Penny. I'm sure you'd rather do that than trim rosebushes anyway, in spite of the fun."

"No! Please!" Penny cried, getting off her bike and putting down the kickstand. "I didn't mean to interfere. I'll just stay here and watch. Okay?"

Faye looked at her mother. "Do we have another pair of trimmers, Mom?" she asked coyly.

"Unfortunately, no," replied her mother, smiling.

"In that case," said Faye, turning back to Penny, "you can watch and take some lessons, all for free. There's a bench under that tree you can sit on."

Penny laughed, went to the bench, and sat down. After a while she began to feel bored. She wanted to discuss with Faye the people she had come here to discuss: Shari and Karen. But she didn't dare to bring up the subject of the girls' super softball playing in Mrs. Marsh's presence. The woman would think that her daughter, and her daughter's friend, had gone bananas.

So, for almost half an hour, Penny sat there and watched them trim rosebushes. Who cared what strains of virus the pregnant Mrs. Nelson had, anyway? Or whether she was going to have two babies, or three? Nothing was more important right now than finding out what had happened to the two girls on the Tall Oaks Hawks softball team.

FIVE

THE HAWKS PRACTICED on one of the four softball fields at the Municipal Athletic Center on Saturday afternoon, a hot, eighty-eight-degree, you-can-fry-an-egg-on-the-sidewalk kind of day. But one player was missing: Faye Marsh.

"Got any idea why Faye isn't here, Penny?" Coach Parker asked, probably knowing that the two girls were close friends.

"No, I don't. And I just saw her Thursday evening," Penny replied, puzzled.

Faye had not even given her a hint that she would not attend practice today. Perhaps she hadn't known then what she'd be doing two days later. Or maybe she came down with one of those viruses she had been talking about, Penny thought wryly.

"Debbie!" Coach Parker called to a brown-haired girl playing catch. "Take second base for infield practice. Move!"

"Yes, *sir!*"

Debbie Brohill, one of the Hawks' three substitutes, broke into a run from near the dugout to the infield, her long, skinny legs flying. If she could hit and catch as well as she could run, Penny was sure the coach would have her start every game instead of Faye. Maybe she'll develop in those areas, Penny thought, and give Faye something to worry about.

"Okay, everybody at their positions!" the coach ordered, picking up a softball and a bat from a pile near the dugout and going to the plate. "Outfielders to the boondocks! Jack Grayson will hit them out to you!"

Jack Grayson, a tall, dark-haired kid wearing a letter-sweater with a TO on it — for Tall Oaks — was a high school athlete who sometimes helped Coach Parker out with fielding practice. He picked up a bat and went to the right side of the plate to hit flies to the outfielders.

Penny glanced across at Karen and tried

to catch her gaze, but Karen seemed absolutely aloof. Penny thought she'd say something to her anyway before the coach started the practice.

"Hi, Karen! How you doing?"

Karen looked at her, her face blank. "Fine, thanks," she said, and focused her attention back on the coach.

"Good," Penny replied, but hardly loud enough for Karen to hear her. I just don't understand it, she thought. Karen's acting exactly as she had during the game on Thursday.

"Okay, Penny!" Coach Parker yelled. "Get one!"

He knocked a fast, bouncing ball down to her, which she fielded perfectly and whipped over to first. Jean Zacks, standing with one foot on the bag, caught it and threw the ball home. Shari caught it, shot it to Penny, and Penny pegged it back to her.

The routine continued with Karen next, then Debbie, and so on, and was repeated several times before Coach Parker decided that his infielders had had enough.

"Okay, twice around the field," he commanded. "Then take off."

Whew! Penny thought, feeling hot, achy,

and tired from the grueling practice. What does he want to do? Kill us?

But they all made the run, and none died from it.

Penny thought about calling Faye after she got home from practice and took a shower. If Faye had come down with some virus, she would appreciate a word or two of sympathy. Especially from her best friend.

But nobody answered the phone on Faye's end when Penny called. Even after ten rings. Maybe she wasn't ill after all, Penny thought. Maybe she and her parents went shopping. Or to visit friends.

Penny didn't see Faye again until the Hawks–Hard Hats game on Tuesday afternoon.

"Hey! How you doing?" Penny cried, rushing over to Faye and grabbing her hands.

Faye stood and looked at her. Faye didn't have the familiar smile on her face that Penny expected to see. Or that pink glow in her cheeks, that gleam in her eyes. She was totally expressionless. Emotionless. "Hi, Penny," she said, robotlike.

Penny stared at her, feeling a tingling in

her arms, a shiver shooting through her body like a weak charge of electricity.

"Faye," she whispered softly, "are you all right?"

Only Faye's lips moved. "I'm okay," she said. Her voice was lukewarm. Almost cold.

Fear gripped Penny. Oh, no! she thought. *Not you, too, Faye! Not you, my best friend!*

"Faye! What's happened to you?" she cried, tension seizing her. "Please tell me! What's changed you?"

Before Penny could say more, Faye, silent, yanked her hands out of Penny's and headed briskly toward the dugout.

SIX

THE HARD HATS HAD FIRST BATS, and June Cato, their leadoff hitter, cracked out a double on the first pitch. Coach Parker had Mary Ann Dru pitching again for the Hawks, because, Penny figured, it had been five days since she had pitched a game and it wouldn't hurt her arm. She had more speed and better control than Edie Moser, the Hawks' other pitcher, and was even a little better at the plate. Edie would pitch on Thursday.

"Bear down, Mary Ann!" Penny shouted from third. "Bear down!"

The Hard Hats' Effie Moon drove a Texas leaguer over short that sure looked as if it were going for a hit. But Karen raced out beyond the bare ground of the infield, stretched her gloved hand far out in front of her, and made the catch.

The crowd went wild.

I can't believe it, Penny thought. She really robbed that batter of a hit!

T. K. Ellis walked on five pitches, bringing up Barbara Nelson, the Hard Hats' home-run queen. The outfielders moved back about five or six steps each, and even Penny stepped back on the grass.

Barbara connected solidly with a hot grounder toward short. Karen scooped it up and shot it to Faye covering second base, and Faye relayed it to first. Penny thought it was the fastest double play she'd ever seen the girls pull off.

"Beautiful fielding, Karen!" she exclaimed as the girls ran off the field together. "Both plays were terrific!"

"Thanks," Karen said, again as deadpan as if she made such catches in every game.

"Blast it, Kim Soo!" a fan yelled as Kim Soo Hong led off for the Hawks. Coach Parker had changed the lineup slightly in this game, according to Harold Dempsey's announcement of the first three batters a moment ago: "Hong! Farrell! Keech!" Penny stood in the on-deck circle, waiting for her turn to bat.

Kim Soo missed the first pitch, then corked a double to right center field.

"Bring her in, Penny!" a fan yelled from the stands behind the backstop screen. Penny recognized Jonny Keech's voice, and a nervous feeling swept over her as she stepped into the batting box. Knowing that Jonny was back there made her think of Karen, and thinking of Karen's brilliant playing tightened the tension even more.

Penny popped two pitches foul, then struck out.

"That's okay, Penny!" she heard Jonny yell. "Better luck next time!"

Sure, she thought. And probably strike out then, too.

She sat down and somehow wasn't surprised when Karen unleashed a hit that went for three bases, scoring Kim Soo. Nothing extraordinary that Karen or Shari did would surprise her anymore.

She glanced down the length of the dugout at Faye, who was sitting at the far end, watching Sophie Kowalski striding to the plate. Wonder where the coach has her batting in the lineup? thought Penny, and then she looked for Harold. She almost jumped with surprise when she saw that he was sitting right next to her.

"Harold, who does Faye bat after?" Penny asked him calmly.

"Mary Ann," he answered, and looked at her apologetically. "I understand you and everybody else were wondering why Faye wasn't at practice last Saturday afternoon," he said in that deep, drawling voice of his.

Penny looked at him. "That's right. Do *you* know where she was?"

"With me."

"What?"

"She went to a movie with me," Harold explained quietly. "Don't look so strange. I've taken Shari and Karen, too. Anyway, we thought we'd get out in time for her to go to practice, but it was a long picture. By the time we got out —"

Penny found herself staring at him and not listening to the rest of what he was saying. She could see her twin images in the mirrors of his dark-brown eyes, see his lips moving, hear the hum of his voice drumming into her ears. But his words were not registering.

Suddenly she didn't like the sight of Harold Dempsey anymore and wanted to get up and find another place to sit. Something about him was frightening her. Something — but she didn't know what.

Penny tried to dismiss Harold from her mind, and she watched as Sophie popped out to second base and Jean Zacks, the first baseman, walked up to the plate. Jean was tall, dark-haired, and left-handed, and almost always when she'd hit the ball would drive it out to left field. This time she drove a hot grounder down to short, which the Hard Hats' shortstop let go through her legs. Karen scored on the error.

Then Mary Ann got up, and Penny saw Faye leave the dugout, pick up a bat, and go to the on-deck circle. Faye picked up one of the metal "doughnuts" that were lying on the ground, slipped it over the handle of her bat, and began swinging the bat back and forth over her shoulders. The doughnut slid down to the heavier part of the bat, giving it extra weight so that it would feel lighter to her while batting.

But Mary Ann grounded out to first for the third out, and Penny would have to wait till the next inning to see what Faye would do.

She didn't have to wait long. Helen Chang grounded out. Her sister, Rose, singled but got out in a double play on a sharp drive to short, and the half-inning was over. *But that double play. So swift and accurate.* Penny couldn't believe it.

Now we'll see how and what Faye does at bat, Penny thought as the Hawks ran off the field.

Faye, leading off the top half of the second inning, swung at the first pitch, a fast ball down by her knees. She met it squarely and the ball shot between third and short for a sharp single. Nothing spectacular, Penny thought, but Faye *had* hit it pretty hard.

Shari, up next, didn't waste any time, either. She also swung at the first pitch, delivering it out to right center for a stand-up double, scoring Faye, who, Penny noticed, ran around the base paths as if a swarm of bees were chasing her.

The run was the only one the Hawks scored that inning, but it put them farther ahead, 3 to 0.

Penny couldn't help but glance at Harold

after Faye had crossed the plate, and see the faint smile on his face as he wrote in the scorebook. Was there another meaning behind that smile, besides the fact that Faye had scored a run? A gleam of satisfaction, maybe? Of triumph? Was Faye's performance *expected?*

What was in that mind of Harold Dempsey's — the computer expert — anyway? What was he thinking of as he wrote the "single" and "run scored" signs in the scorebook after Faye's name?

Harold Dempsey. *Where had he taken Faye and the other two girls, after they had left the movies those Saturday afternoons?*

SEVEN

PENNY, standing on the ground behind and to the side of the third-base sack and just inside of the short-cut grass, waited for the Hard Hats' leadoff girl to come to the plate. But her mind was still on Harold and the three girls, Shari, Karen, and Faye. What could she do? Now that her closest friend, Faye, was also under that strange spell — Penny couldn't think of anything else to call it — whom could she talk to? Who would believe her? You would think that other members on the team could *see* that something had turned those girls into strangers and superstars, but no one else had mentioned it. Maybe some of them had noticed it but were reluctant to say so. As I am reluctant, Penny thought. *But someone has got to say something to somebody sometime!*

Joyce Buddins, the Hard Hats left center fielder, corked a single over short, and the next two girls got out, both on fly balls to the outfield. Then June Cato, the top of the Hard Hats' lineup, came up again and drove a hot grounder down to third. Watching it come at her in short, rapid hops, Penny knew she was going to miss it. She felt too tense and nervous.

And miss it she did. The ball struck the heel of her glove, hit her on the chest, and bounced to the ground. By the time she retrieved it, June was almost on first base — too late for Penny to throw there — and Joyce was on second.

"Sorry," Penny said apologetically to Mary Ann as she tossed the ball to the pitcher.

"Forget it," said Mary Ann. "That came at you like a bullet."

She doesn't know that I missed it because I wasn't concentrating on my playing, Penny thought guiltily.

Effie Moon knocked a high bouncer down to third. Penny caught it easily and stepped on the bag for the force-out. She caught Mary Ann's smile as the girls ran off the field together. "I needed that," Penny said, feeling better.

She reached the dugout and was about to sit down when she heard Harold calling out the names of the first three batters. "Farrell! Keech! Kowalski!" Oh, no! she thought, forgetting that Kim Soo had made the last out in the bottom of the second inning.

Penny dropped her glove on the bench, walked to the pile of bats, selected her favorite yellow one, and went to the plate. She felt nervous and hot. A lot of things were on her mind. That error, for one, in spite of her redeeming herself on the next grounder hit down to her. The three girls. Harold. And her striking out her first time up.

She let the first pitch sail by. "Strike!" cried the umpire, a six-foot, broad-shouldered guy towering behind the catcher.

Who can I talk with about it? Penny asked herself. Who can I confide in?

She was tempted to swing at the next pitch, but wasn't ready.

"Strike two!" boomed the umpire.

"Relax, Penny!" Coach Parker's voice drifted to her from the third-base coaching box. "Just meet it!"

Penny stepped out of the box, shut her eyes tightly for a few seconds, took a deep breath, then opened her eyes and got back in the box again. The next pitch was a fast one that zoomed up near her shoulders. She swung at it, and missed.

The cheer from the Hard Hats' fans hit her as if it were a physical thing, and she returned to the dugout, not looking up once till she got there.

"It's only a ball game, Penny," Melanie Fallon said to her as she gave Penny room to sit beside her. "Don't feel so bad."

"I guess I just can't help it," said Penny, her heart pounding.

Cries from other team members began exploding from the dugout. "Get on, Karen! Get on!"

"Another long clout, Karen!"

Karen lashed out a single.

Sophie came up next, and doubled. And Karen, who Penny thought would hold up at third base, raced all the way in to score.

"Oh, wow!" Melanie exclaimed. "Can she *run!*"

Penny looked at her, wondering. "Have you noticed how much *faster* she's been running lately? And how much *better* she's been playing?"

"Who hasn't?" Melanie replied. She had her cap tipped back, revealing her short, blond hair that partially covered her ears. Her blue eyes were wide, enhanced by her long lashes. "You'd think she was getting tips from some big-leaguer or something."

Penny looked harder at her. Maybe I can confide in *her,* she suddenly thought. Melanie was eleven, sensible, and smart. She'd understand.

"Can I talk to you after the game, Melanie?" Penny asked, making sure only Melanie heard her.

Melanie stared at her, frowning. "Sure."

Penny smiled, a wave of relief sweeping over her. At last, she thought. Even if Melanie couldn't help her solve the problem, Penny at least could share her views with someone. Talking with her mother or father, or with both of them, was out of the question, Penny had decided. They didn't know any of the girls half as well as she did, and they wouldn't be able to compare the girls' present behavior with their past.

It would seem that their own parents, or their brothers and sisters — especially Karen's brother Jonny — would recognize the change in them, Penny thought. But, so far, none of them had said anything. Were they so naïve as to think that whatever it was that had changed the girls was temporary? Or that it wasn't serious? Maybe someday I'll find the answer myself, Penny thought. I just hope that by then it won't be too late.

Too late for what? she asked herself. But how could she know what would finally happen? *What if, whatever it was, had already happened?*

Penny was so absorbed in her thoughts that she didn't see what the next two batters did. Not till she saw Faye leaving the on-deck circle for the plate did she notice Mary Ann on first base.

"How'd Mary Ann get on?" Penny asked Kim Soo, sitting on the other side of her.

"Jean grounded out to short, and the shortstop missed Mary Ann's grounder," Kim Soo answered, flashing one of her bright, eye-sparkling smiles. "Aren't you watching the game, Penny?"

Penny shrugged. "I guess I wasn't paying much attention to it," she admitted.

She focused her attention on Faye now, and saw her take two pitches, both almost hitting the plate. Then Faye swung at the third pitch so hard that one would think she was trying to smash the softball into pieces. The sound of bat meeting ball was solid, and almost instantly a roar exploded from the crowd as the ball soared out to deep center field. Everyone in the Hawks dugout stood up — stunned silent — as the ball cleared the fence by at least thirty feet for one of the longest home runs ever hit there.

The team cheered and applauded, and then each member of it dashed out of the dugout and up to the plate to shake Faye's hands — both of them — as she crossed the plate behind Sophie and Mary Ann. Penny met her eyes, and for a moment their eyes were locked as Penny said, "Beautiful hit, Faye. It was just fantastic."

"Thanks," Faye said.

"Thanks." That was all. She never even cracked a smile.

Penny saw Faye go down toward the end of the dugout and sit next to Karen, and looked to see if there was room on the other side of Faye. There was. Penny then got up, walked down to the vacant spot, and sat down.

She looked at Faye. "Faye, I've got to talk to you," she whispered.

Faye looked at her. Her eyes were blank. "I don't want to talk," she said.

"Faye! We have to!"

Faye looked at her a moment longer, and nothing on her face or in her eyes suggested she was interested in what Penny wanted to say. "I told you, I don't want to talk," she said again, and looked away.

Just then there was an explosive roar from the fans, and Penny looked up in time to see Shari thrown out at first base. The third inning was over. Hard Hats 0, Hawks 7.

T. K. Ellis, a tall, spindly-legged girl, led off the top of the fourth inning for the Hard Hats and dumped a Texas leaguer over second base. Barbara Nelson then tripled, scoring T. K. Helen Chang homered, and the Hard Hats' fans went crazy.

Then Mary Ann walked the next two girls, and Penny began to wonder: Aren't we ever going to get them out? Isn't the *thing* that's happened to Shari, Karen, and Faye enough?

She realized that in her uppermost thoughts she was hoping for the Hawks to win, momentarily forgetting that they had been doing so well only because of the change — the superstar qualities — that the three girls had mysteriously acquired. If she had a choice, what would she want? A winning team, or to have her friends return to their normal selves?

Wow! she thought. What am I thinking? The *girls* come first! I want them to be normal again! Winning comes second.

EIGHT

JOYCE BUDDINS, the Hard Hats' tall, freckle-faced left center fielder, got her second single of the game, a sharp drive over third base, scoring Rose Chang. Rose and Cay Lattimore were the two girls Mary Ann had walked in succession after that home run by Helen Chang. Cay stopped on third.

"Wait a minute! Time!" Penny yelled to the base umpire, and trotted in to the pitcher's mound, hoping to say something to Mary Ann to calm her down. Jean came in from first base, too, but Karen and Faye remained at their positions at the edge of the infield grass, and Shari behind the plate, as if their presence wasn't needed. Penny wasn't surprised that they didn't come. Whatever it was that had made them become almost one hundred percent emotionless had made them less considerate about certain things, too. Always before they used to come to the mound with Penny and Jean when their pitcher needed that much-welcomed moral support. That *it* — whatever it was — had changed all that.

"Slow down," Penny advised Mary Ann. "Take a breather."

She could see that the girl was sweating profusely, moving about every second, looking this way and that like a worried bird. Suddenly Penny heard feet pounding behind her and turned to see Coach Parker running toward them from the dugout. He was looking back over his shoulder at a girl warming up in the bullpen. When the girl, Edie Moser, looked up, he signaled for her to come in. She tossed the ball to the girl she was playing catch with, and came running out to the field.

"I guess I should've put Edie in right after Chang knocked that home run," the coach admitted to Mary Ann. "But you were doing so well before that, I hated to take you out."

Mary Ann smiled, and shrugged. "I guess

I started to get nervous," she said shyly. She handed him the ball and ran off the field, receiving applause and cheers from the fans till she disappeared into the dugout.

Edie threw a few underhand pitches in to Shari, Coach Parker left the infield, Penny and Jean returned to their positions, and the game resumed. Annie Moses, the Hard Hats' batter, laced Edie's first pitch in the gap between left and left center fields for three bases, scoring two runs, and Penny wondered again whether the inning was ever going to end. Had that crazy spell touched the Hard Hats, too?

Then Pam Colt, the Hard Hats pitcher, drove a sharp grounder to Karen, who caught the ball easily and whipped it in a straight line to Jean for the putout. The next batter grounded out to Penny, and the third flied out to Gloria in right center field to end the Hard Hats' big inning. Hard Hats 6, Hawks 7.

The score remained the same until the bottom of the sixth inning, when Faye connected with a double over the shortstop's head, followed by another double by Shari. Both hits were solid line drives that were hit directly at the outfielders, but not high enough for them to catch the balls in the air. Any other girl — including me, Penny thought — would not have risked running to second base. But both Faye and Shari had stretched their hits to doubles.

Melanie grounded out to short. Then Gloria singled, scoring Shari, and Kim Soo singled, driving Gloria all around to third base. Penny popped out to short — *disgusting,* she thought — ending the half-inning, and the Hawks led by three runs.

"Don't let it get you down, Penny," Harold said, smiling, as Penny came into the dugout for her glove. "We're ahead."

She wanted to ignore him; there was something about him — something strange — that bothered her. She couldn't describe the feeling, but it was there.

Yet she couldn't ignore him. What if she was wrong? What if she just *thought* there was something strange about him because he was a nut about computers, and had taken all three of the changed girls to the movies? Wasn't it quite a coincidence that it happened to be *those* girls?

Penny inhaled deeply as she swooped up

her glove and shot a quick glance at him. "I'll try not to, Harold," she promised, and ran out to her position at third.

Why should I feel so strange now whenever I'm near him, or when he speaks to me? she wondered. Am I going crazy, or what?

The Hard Hats' bats went wild again in the top half of the seventh inning and didn't stop until five runs had crossed the plate, including two home runs — both by the Chang sisters. Penny, running in toward the dugout, her legs and shoulders aching from the long, tough game, couldn't believe it. Those darned Hard Hats just won't give up! she thought.

Well, we won't either, she murmured quietly to herself as she plopped down on the bench. Her heart wasn't entirely into winning the game now. The *thing* that had happened to the girls took first consideration.

"Start it off, Karen!" a familiar voice yelled from the bench. "Belt it out of the lot!"

Harold's voice. Penny saw Karen going to the plate, carrying her bat as if it were a toothpick. Karen stepped into the batter's box, rubbed the toes of her sneakers into the dirt till she was comfortable in her stance, and faced the pitcher. Pam Colt stood on the mound, tall and erect, holding the softball in front of her with both hands. Then she whipped the ball underhand with her right, and it sailed in toward the plate in a fast, shallow arc.

Boom! Karen swung and met it solidly. The ball zoomed to deep left center field and over the fence for a home run, her third hit of the game.

"I knew she'd do it!" Harold exclaimed, his face beaming as he printed "HR" in the seventh-inning box opposite Karen's name in the scorebook. "I knew it!"

Penny shot him a cold, questioning look. Mary Ann was sitting between them, but Penny had to say what was on her mind. She couldn't resist it. "*How* did you know, Harold?" she asked softly.

He finished writing in the scorebook and glanced up at her. He was still beaming, still flushed with having guessed that Karen was going to hit a home run. "I don't know. I guess I just *felt* it," he said.

"Sure," Penny replied, her voice low, almost inaudible.

"I beg your pardon?"

"Nothing," Penny said, turning away from

him. She could see him looking at her, and Mary Ann looking at her, and felt a chill ripple along her spine. Don't give me that dumb, I-don't-know-what-you're-talking-about look, Harold, she wanted to tell him. You know very well what I'm talking about.

Sophie Kowalski singled over short, then got out on a double play as Jean ripped a fast one-bouncer down to second base. Edie walked and Faye came up. Silent, Penny waited for Harold to yell for her to belt one out of the lot, too. The thought had scarcely come to her mind when his voice boomed, "Out of the lot, Faye! Go after it, girl!"

Tense, Penny waited to see what Faye would do. Faye let the first pitch go by; it was too low. She let the next one go by; it was also too low.

"Make it be in there, Faye!" Coach Parker's advice came from the third-base coaching box.

Two-and-nothing. Faye should let the next pitch go by, too, whether or not it was going to be a strike, Penny thought. If it was a strike, Faye would still have two chances left to hit. If it was a ball, the chances were better that the next pitch would be a ball and she'd draw a walk.

The pitch came in. It was a good one, and Faye swung at it. She walloped it hard into right center field and stopped on second base for a stand-up double. Edie held up at third.

"Way to go, Faye!" Harold cried, his face beaming again as he made the proper notation in the scorebook. Penny could not resist glancing in his direction to see the expression on his face.

"The winning run's on second, Shari!" Harold yelled then. "Get a hit, Shari! A hit will do it!"

Shari stepped into the box, took three pitches, then slammed a waist-high pitch between the right and left center fielders for a stand-up double. The hit drove in Edie and Faye, ending the ball game, with the Hawks winning it, 12 to 11.

Penny found herself cheering with all the other members of the team and the Hawks' fans, but her heart wasn't in it. *It wasn't Shari who had hit that ball,* she told herself. *It wasn't Faye who had hit hers, and it wasn't Karen who had hit that home run. Something had taken over their bodies. And there was one person who knew what it was: Harold Dempsey!*

NINE

"PENNY!"

Penny had left the dugout and was running to catch up with Melanie when she heard the voice. She stopped running, turned, and stared in surprise at the stout, slightly bow-legged boy sprinting toward her, the scorebook clasped tightly against his side.

"Yes, Harold?" she asked as he came up beside her, puffing slightly.

That beaming face again! Was he mocking her?

"I'd like to ask you something," he said.

"Oh?" She started to walk on, hoping to reach Melanie at the gate. At the same time, she didn't want to be left alone with Harold.

She had become frightened of him. She was sure now he was responsible for Karen's, Shari's, and Faye's strange behavior and abnormal athletic abilities. She had questions to ask him, too, but she wasn't prepared to spring them on him now.

She stared at him. "What is it you want to ask me, Harold?" she said, trying to keep her voice under control.

"Will . . . will you go to a movie with me this Saturday afternoon?" he asked in a soft, pleasant voice. "The one that starts at five P.M., because —"

Penny's hazel eyes widened as she heard his invitation. "You asked me once before, Harold, and I said I couldn't go."

He nodded, his head bobbing as if it were hooked onto a spring. "I know. And you said you were going to be busy that Saturday afternoon. I thought —"

"I'm sorry, Harold," she interrupted. "I mean . . . I don't know. I'll have to see if my mom and dad have anything planned. Okay?"

She had to get out of it somehow. And she didn't want him to think that she suspected him of any villainy. Not now. She felt she would be in danger now.

She flashed him a weak smile. "I'm sorry,"

she said again, and started to run toward the exit, when another voice suddenly called out to her. "Penny! Wait a second!"

She looked over her shoulder to her right and saw that it was Jonny Keech. Jonny! Her heart skipped a beat. She almost failed to see that Karen was with him. His head was bare, and his blond hair was tossing about like corn tassels in the wind. There was a humorous glint in his blue eyes as he and Karen came forward, and Penny wondered if it was because they had seen her talking with Harold.

"What? Walking home alone?" Jonny asked, cracking a smile that flashed brilliant white teeth and deep dimples in his cheeks.

Penny shrugged. "I was going to walk home with Melanie," she said, glancing toward the gate where Melanie was waiting for her. "But — " She paused and looked at him, smiling shyly, because she didn't know what to say to him in front of Karen.

Suddenly Karen broke away in a run, her hair flying in the wind as she headed toward the exit and shouted over her shoulder, "See you at home, Jonny!"

"Okay!" Jonny yelled back to her, waving, then looked back at Penny, his eyes bluer than ever as Penny gazed into them. She could hardly believe that he had called to her, that he was now standing only inches away from her. He was slightly taller than she, and was wearing a white t-shirt that showed off his tanned arms. "Some game," he said.

"Sure was," she agreed.

They started toward the gate, walking slowly. Suddenly Penny remembered Harold, and she looked back and saw him disappearing behind the backstop screen where there was another exit.

She turned and caught Jonny looking at her. Amusement sparkled in his blue eyes. "Saw Harold talking to you. Interesting guy, isn't he?"

She smiled. "He sure is."

"What did he want? No, never mind," he added quickly. "It's not any of my business."

"Oh, that's okay," Penny said, willing to tell him. "He just asked me if I'd go to a movie with him this Saturday afternoon, and I said I couldn't."

"Oh?" He laughed. "He took Karen a couple of weeks ago, you know."

"Yes, I know," Penny replied. "And Faye last Saturday afternoon."

"Oh?" Jonny's eyebrows arched. "He sure gets around, doesn't he?"

"I guess he does." Penny wanted to elaborate, to say more about Harold, but felt that it would be unwise to tell Jonny what she suspected. So far she had no proof that Harold was responsible for the girls' — Shari's, Karen's, and Faye's — superstar qualities in the infield and at the plate. Once she was sure of it, she'd mention it to Jonny. Till then she would remain silent about it.

Unless he brought it up first.

"Maybe *we* can go sometime," he suggested.

She stared at him, surprised, and felt her cheeks turning hot. "Maybe," she said. Her heart pounded. Was she having a dream? "I'd like that," she added.

They arrived at the gate, and Penny saw that Melanie had started to walk on ahead, as if she didn't want to intrude in their private conversation.

"I think Melanie's waiting for you," Jonny observed, his blue eyes flashing at her again. "I'll see you, then . . . soon. Okay?"

"Okay," she said, trying hard to hide her excitement. She didn't want him to know how really pleased she was that he had called to her and walked with her even *this* far.

"Bye," he said, and ran off, saying hi to Melanie as he swept past her down the sidewalk, his blond hair bobbing with each smooth, graceful stride.

"Well, what was all that about?" Melanie asked as Penny reached her side. "And don't tell me 'nothin',' because that look in your eyes says it was 'somethin'.' "

Penny smiled. "Believe it or not, it was practically nothing. But" — she sighed — "there's hope."

"What did that twerp Harold want?" Melanie asked as they walked along.

"He invited me to go with him to a movie this Saturday afternoon. How about that?"

"Great!" Melanie's eyes widened, interested. "You said you'd go, didn't you?"

"No. I hedged, then I said I couldn't."

"What? Dummy! Why not? He's paying for it, isn't he? The inviter *always* pays."

"Yes, but I gave him some crazy excuse, something about Mom and Dad probably having plans for Saturday afternoon."

"You're crazy, Penny Farrell," Melanie snapped. "You know that? Wish he had asked me. I wouldn't have hedged. I would've said,

'Sure, buster. What time you picking me up?' " Penny laughed. "You said you wanted to talk to me after the game," Melanie went on. "What do you want to talk about?"

Penny's eyes fixed on hers. "The girls — Shari, Karen, and Faye."

"What about them?"

"What about them?" Penny's eyes widened. "Don't tell me you haven't noticed how weird they've been acting! They're like superathletes! And cold and emotionless as sticks!"

Melanie frowned. "Come to think of it, yes. I noticed how well they were playing. And now that you mention their attitude . . ." She stared at Penny. "That *is* strange, isn't it?"

"Sure it is," Penny said. "And what is equally strange is that Harold Dempsey took all three of those girls to movies the last three Saturdays!"

"Hmm. But that could be a coincidence, couldn't it, Penny?" said Melanie, her forehead knitted.

"It could be. But think. What positions do those girls play?"

Melanie thought. Then her eyes widened again. "They're all infielders!" she exclaimed. "And now he's invited *you* — also an infielder — to a movie!"

"Right. Don't you think it sounds like a plan to you? A weird sort of plan?"

Melanie nodded. "It sure does. But how could he be responsible for what's happened to the girls? That sounds pretty far-fetched, doesn't it?"

"Sure it does. But so did the airplane when the Wright Brothers told somebody about it," said Penny. "And, don't forget, Harold's a computer whiz. Who knows what he can do?"

"Yeah," said Melanie, her mind seemingly miles away.

"Know what?" Penny went on, thinking deeply. "I'm going to find out more about that little scorekeeper friend of ours. I'm going to take your suggestion and accept his invitation. But it's not the movie I'm interested in. It's what happens *afterward*."

Melanie smiled broadly. "Right! And if you find out anything, let me know! Will you?"

"Of course, I will."

Melanie grabbed Penny's hands in both of hers. "This sounds like real detective work,

Penny!" she said excitedly. "Can I be your sidekick?"

"No," said Penny seriously. "I've got to do this myself, Mel, and make sure he doesn't get suspicious." She heaved a sigh of relief, flung her arms around her friend, and exclaimed, "Oh, I feel so relieved! I had to talk to someone, Mel, and I couldn't think of anyone better than you! You're a peach!"

"Thanks," Melanie said evenly. "But I hope that neither of us turns out to be a fruitcake."

Penny laughed.

That evening she telephoned Harold and got him on the first ring. He was probably home alone, she thought, or had a phone right next to his computer.

"Harold Dempsey speaking."

"Hi, Harold. This is Penny."

"Oh! Hi, Penny! Well, this is sure a surprise."

Penny smiled. "Yes, I suppose it is," she said. "Anyway, that invitation you offered me today? About going to a movie?"

"Oh, I'm *so* sorry, Penny." Harold's deep, drawling voice sounded sincere. "But I've already asked Gloria to go with me."

Penny's throat went dry. Gloria? Gloria Johnson? "Oh." She tried not to sound too disappointed.

"Look! Maybe I can cancel it. I can tell her —"

"No. Don't do that," Penny cut in. "You take Gloria. It's . . . okay."

"Maybe next week?" Harold asked hopefully.

"Maybe," said Penny, her voice barely audible. "So long, Harold."

She hung up, staring at the floor, her nerves strung tight as violin strings. Gloria was an outfielder. Harold's taking her to a movie was breaking the pattern. All the other girls who had "changed" were infielders. But he was willing to break his date with Gloria and take me, Penny thought. And I'm an infielder.

Was Gloria going to be one of his victims even though she was an outfielder? Or would Harold wait now till next week, to see if Penny would go to a movie with him or not?

Penny closed her eyes tightly and shuddered.

TEN

GLORIA HAD TO BE WARNED about Harold, Penny thought, the urgency of it making her more nervous than ever. If Gloria agreed to go to a movie with him, okay. If she agreed to go to a fast-food restaurant with him, okay. But she should go home immediately afterwards. If Harold invited her to his home after that, she *had* to refuse. That was it. Otherwise . . .

Her hands trembling, Penny picked up the phone book, found Gloria's number, and dialed it. Mrs. Johnson answered.

"This is Penny Farrell," said Penny, trying to keep from sounding worried. "May I speak to Gloria, please?"

"I'm sorry, Penny," Mrs. Johnson replied in her pleasant, high-pitched voice. "But Gloria's gone for the day. She's going to spend today and most of tomorrow with her aunt in Fort Mill."

"Oh?" Penny was so disappointed at the news she was speechless for a minute.

"Can I give her a message when she gets home?" Mrs. Johnson asked.

"No. No, thank you. It's not important. Thank you, Mrs. Johnson. Goodbye."

"Is anything wrong, dear?" Mrs. Johnson hastened to ask before Penny could hang up. Something in Penny's tone must have hinted to her that something was bothering the girl.

"No." Penny laughed. "Nothing's wrong at all, Mrs. Johnson. Goodbye."

She hung up the phone, and stared again at the floor. What was she going to do now?

A voice jarred her thoughts. "Penny. Is something wrong? You look as if the world's problems have all been suddenly dumped onto your shoulders."

Penny glanced up and saw her mother peering anxiously at her from the kitchen doorway. She had on a light jacket, as if she were ready to go out.

Penny forced a smile. Should she tell her mother about her suspicions? How could she, and make it sound convincing? She had told Melanie, but now that her plan to go to a movie with Harold had gone awry, she had to tell someone else. And soon.

Her mother came into the room, put a hand on Penny's shoulder, and smiled. "I don't have much time. I have to leave for a dentist's appointment. But, if there's something that's bothering you . . ."

Penny looked at her. "Mom, is it possible for somebody with a computer to . . . to learn something from it to be able to change the behavior of people, and turn them into . . . superathletes?"

Her mother's brown eyes looked serious for a moment, then suddenly changed to amusement. "Oh, darling! Your imagination can certainly take off at times!" She put her hand on Penny's shoulder and looked into her eyes. "A computer can do a lot of things, but change the behavior of people? Turn them into superathletes?" She shook her head. "It sounds impossible to me. That's not something I'd ever worry about, honey." She leaned forward, kissed Penny on the forehead, and smiled. "Well, I've got to run.

Leave a note if you're going anywhere, okay?"

"I will."

Penny watched her mother leave, then sat there awhile, wishing she hadn't said a word to her. Speaking to someone about her suspicions wouldn't get her anywhere until she had some proof.

But there had to be someone who would listen. Someone who would believe . . .

Jonny! Why not? At least he would listen. He was intelligent, more intelligent than a lot of kids his age. And understanding. She had to tell him. And now. She couldn't delay it any longer.

Her hands trembling, she picked up the phone book again, looked for Jonny's number, found it, and dialed it. The line was busy. She waited a few minutes and tried again. Still busy.

Penny felt *sure* that she could trust Jonny and talk to him confidentially. She decided not to wait any longer for the phone to ring. She raced to the bathroom, ran the brush through her dark hair about a dozen times, checked her pink blouse and blue skirt in the full-length mirror, left a note for her mother, and left. She rode her bike, because the sooner she got to Jonny's and told him about Harold, the quicker something could be done — *if* something could be done — to make him stop it. *Correcting* whatever he'd done to the girls was something else again. But that, too, had to be reckoned with. Maybe Jonny would know what to do.

It was still hot even though it was late in the afternoon, and by the time Penny had pumped her bike the four blocks to Meadow Street, where the Keeches lived, flecks of perspiration glistened on her forehead and above her mouth. She left the bike standing up on its kickstand next to the steps leading to the Keeches' front porch, lifted up her hair in back to free it from sticking to her neck, and approached the front door. Her heart was pounding.

She was just about to ring the doorbell when the door opened and a girl came out, a pretty, dark-haired girl with an oval face and a small mole on her left cheek. Jean Zacks. The Hawks second baseman.

Penny froze as she stared at the masklike face of the girl before her. There was something about Jean that immediately reminded Penny of the other infielders who had been supercharged by, Penny thought, Harold Dempsey's computer. But this was Jonny Keech's house, not Harold's. And the boy standing directly behind Jean — the smile on his face suddenly disappearing — was Jonny himself.

ELEVEN

JONNY STARED over Jean's shoulder at Penny, a surprised look coming over his face.

"Penny!" he exclaimed, the tone of his usually velvety voice matching the surprise on his face.

Penny looked from Jean to him. Jean glanced at her. "Hi, Penny," she said, her voice flat and wooden, as she walked out the door past Penny to the street. Penny watched her until she turned left at the sidewalk in the direction of her home. Then she looked back at Jonny, feeling rooted to the porch but wanting to run away, to put as much distance between her and Jonny as she could.

Suddenly she feared him as much as she had liked him before. And all the time she had blamed Harold for what had been happening to the girls!

"Penny," Jonny said again. "Hello." He said the words haltingly and guiltily. Their eyes locked.

"So it was you all the time," Penny said accusingly. "You're the one who's been turning those girls, including your own sister, into heartless wonders."

"No," he said, his gaze unwavering. "That is . . ." He hesitated, looking away.

"That is *what?* I just saw Jean Zacks walking out of here looking like . . . like a robot!" Penny thundered. "How can you explain *that?*"

Jonny's face paled. Penny could see that he was fighting his emotions: he knew he was guilty for doing what he had done, but hated to admit it.

"I didn't do it," he said, his voice almost quavering. "I mean, I'm not really responsible for what happened."

Penny frowned. "You're *not?* Then who is, Jonny?" she asked, her voice rising. "*Who is?*"

"Well . . . I mean . . . Harold."

"Harold?" Her eyes widened. "How?"

Jonny's mouth opened, closed. He looked away from her, at the floor, the walls, as if searching for the right answer to give her.

"How, Jonny?" Penny repeated. "How could Harold in any way be responsible? Are you two working together in this . . . this *monstrous* thing?"

"Well, sort of."

"How?"

"It was Harold's computer," Jonny answered slowly. "My dad bought it from him about a month ago."

"That *still* doesn't make it Harold's fault," Penny said, "unless I'm missing something here."

"Well, I mean . . . if my dad hadn't ever bought the thing, and I hadn't started fooling around with it . . ." His voice trailed off.

"I *thought* a computer was involved in this thing," Penny said, her shock over Jonny's involvement conflicting with her satisfaction in knowing that her early hunch was right. "But how could it change people? How could it turn a person into a superathlete, and . . . and deaden their feelings?"

"They're not deadened," Jonny said hastily. "They're just . . . well, sort of relaxed. Weak."

Penny stared at him, suddenly furious. "I can't understand it. How could a simple computer —"

"It's not simple," Jonny cut in. "Harold's father did some work on it, making it more sophisticated than it was before. Then, when Dad bought it for me, I upgraded it more."

She couldn't take her eyes off him. " 'Upgraded it more'?" she echoed, and waited for him to explain.

He nodded. "Look, our air conditioner is on," he said. "It's more comfortable talking inside than it is out there. Do you want to come in?"

Penny hesitated. "I'm not sure."

"There's nothing to be afraid of," he said. "Really."

He stepped back. Then, still a bit cautious, Penny entered the house, and Jonny closed the door behind her. He was right: it was much cooler inside.

"Come on. I'll take you to my computer room," Jonny invited, heading toward a narrow, carpeted hall. "You probably want to see it now that you're here, anyway, I think."

"Yes. I do," Penny replied. "But I don't know whether I should."

Jonny glanced back at her. "I want you to," he insisted. "Please."

He sounded sincere. Penny considered his invitation, and her situation. If he tried to do anything to her — grab her, force her into whatever kind of invention he used for his incredible purpose — she could turn and run. She was a fast runner. She was sure she'd be out of the house and down the street before he was out the door.

"Okay," she said, making sure, though, that there was a gap of several feet between them.

Jonny turned into the open door of his room and Penny followed him in. The moment she stepped across the threshold she stopped, breathless. The room wasn't large, perhaps not more than nine feet square, but every shelf was crammed with books, magazines, and cassettes. Along two walls were the components of a computer. No. *Two* computers, on tables against each wall.

"You can see I've got two monitors and two keyboards," Jonny explained as he stood next to the system across the room from Penny. "This smaller one here is the one Dad bought me a couple of years ago. That set there," he pointed to the larger monitor and keyboard on the table near Penny, "is the one I got from Harold. It's got a dual disk drive, whereas this one is a single disk drive. With two drives you don't have to keep switching disks, like you do with a single. But I guess you know that."

"A little," said Penny, who was learning the fundamentals of computer literacy in school. "But how did you use it to supercharge those girls — or whatever it was you did to them?"

Jonny went to the system that was next to Penny, reached around the monitor, lifted a latch, and pulled down a flap, revealing four sets of inch-wide rubber cups.

Penny stared at them. "They look like electrodes," she exclaimed, "those things they use in lie-detector tests."

"They're similar," said Jonny. He pulled one out and Penny saw that a tube was attached to it. "Put two on each arm, turn on the switch, and you're ready to go," he added, a sly grin coming over his face.

Penny's eyes widened. "That's it? Put two on each arm, turn on the —"

"Not quite," Jonny cut in. "There are certain commands you have to give the computer."

Penny frowned, curious. "Commands? Where did you learn about the commands?"

He looked at her. Once again he was very serious. "I programmed them into the computer."

"*You* programmed them?" Penny felt her spine turning into an icicle, felt herself frozen to the floor. She was afraid Jonny might grab her, sit her down on the chair next to the computer, stick the electrodes onto her arms, and presto! change her into another super player. But he didn't, and she was sure then that he wasn't going to.

"I programmed them," he repeated. "I started with my simpler computer first, about a year ago, experimenting with mice."

"And it worked?" Penny heard her voice sounding almost like a screech. She repeated her question, more softly. "It worked?"

Jonny nodded. "It was a long time before I started to get results, but I had the mice lifting stones five times their own weight."

Penny gulped. "Lifting stones? How?"

Jonny grinned proudly. "First, I took two mice, fastened the electrodes onto their bodies, then, little by little, I began feeding information into the computer."

"What kind of information?"

"Formulas. I took the color graphics program and set up a model of the human body, showing all its muscles." His face beamed. "Then I programmed the voice commands to send electrical vibrations out through these tubes to whatever muscles I highlighted on the screen. But I had to do it in steps, and each step was a separate formula which was able to work only when done in the correct sequence. Follow me?"

Penny's forehead was already knitted. "I don't know," she confessed. "What about the mice? What did you do with them after you stuck the electrodes onto their bodies?"

"I placed hunks of cheese inside a two-inch-square box," Jonny explained. "Then I laid the stone on top of the box and just waited for the mice to get good and hungry."

"And?"

"Well, I experimented with each one separately, to see if the reactions would be the same. And they were. When the mice got good and hungry, they lifted the stone and got the cheese. A stone five times their own weight."

Penny stared at him. The ice around her spine had melted. But she was still cautious, wary. She still could not make herself trust him one hundred percent.

"What happened? Did the mice start bulging with muscles?" she asked, curious.

He chuckled. "No. They just got strong. Their muscles simply became like steel."

"That's why no one could tell that the girls had changed by just looking at them," Penny observed.

"Right," said Jonny.

"But it affected their minds," she said. "Their behavior. How come?"

Jonny shook his head and looked away from her. "I'm not sure. All I can think of is that the change in their bodies caused by the computer must have also created a reaction in their brain waves. I don't think it's anything damaging, or permanent." He started tapping the edge of the computer table nervously with his fingers.

"But you're not sure." It was more a statement than a question.

"Not completely, no."

Penny shook her head, incredulous. "But you must have seen a change in Shari's behavior, Jonny. And in Karen's. Why did

89

you continue with your experiment? Why?"

He shrugged. His face began to look pale, drawn. "I wasn't worried about their behavior. Not at first. I just thought it was a normal, unimportant side effect."

" 'Normal'? 'Unimportant'? You must be kidding!"

"No. I figured it was just tied in with their physical change. That it was just a temporary thing." He met her eyes squarely. "Penny, don't you understand? I was so surprised that the experiment worked I didn't give much thought to the girls' emotions! I know that sounds crazy, but it's true! I really didn't think the experiment would work!"

Penny sucked in a deep breath, let it out, and went on quietly, "Shari was the first girl — victim — you tried it on. Didn't you explain the experiment to her? What might happen to her if it worked?"

"Of course, I did! I explained it to all of them!"

"But none of them — including your own sister, Karen — was a bit worried? Not one bit?"

Jonny shrugged. "Well, Shari was a bit cautious at first. But I picked her because she's a jolly kid. And daring. She wanted to know what the experiment would do to her, if it succeeded, and if it would leave any aftereffects. I told her it should improve her playing ability, but that's all. And that she should be normal again in a week or so."

"But it's lasted longer than that," Penny said. "A lot longer. Jonny, I can't believe you."

Jonny nodded. "Yeah. I know," he murmured. "I can't believe me, either." He sounded sick.

"Why did you do it?" Penny asked. "Why didn't you pick on another animal? A dog, for example. Or a cat?"

He lifted his shoulders. "The Hawks were losing games, that's why. And the infielders were playing the lousiest of anybody. Including you, Penny. Harold and I used to talk about it. And I thought . . . well, if my experiment worked, I would turn Shari into a superplayer first, then, one by one, you other infielders, and the Hawks should start winning. When Karen saw how Shari was playing after I gave her the treatment, I had no trouble convincing her to have it, too. She thought it was fun. And exciting. Well, I did, too. And Harold helped by getting us all together."

"Didn't Karen notice that the treatment

also affected Shari's personality? And worry that it might affect hers the same way?"

"Yes. But I told her it was temporary. Not anything to worry about." He shook his head, and Penny could see that he was really suffering over this now. "I'm really sorry, Penny," he said. "I really am."

"Sorry?" She looked at him squarely. "Sorry won't help, Jonny. The parents of those girls must have noticed that something is different about their daughters by now. If they find out that you're behind it, you'll really be in hot water! Jonny, you've got to change them back, you hear me? You've got to bring those girls back here and turn them into normal human beings again!" Her anger mounted, and she clenched her fists and felt like pounding him on the chest to let him know she meant it. "Do you hear me, Jonny?" Her voice rose in a crescendo as the words left her mouth. "You've got to change those girls back to normal! Now!"

Jonny's face seemed even paler than before, his voice almost inaudible as he stared at her and said, "I can't, Penny. I don't know how."

TWELVE

ALL LIFE SEEMED to drain out of Penny as Jonny's raw, slowly delivered words registered in her mind. She had to find a chair and sit down, she thought, or she'd faint.

A worn cushioned chair with wooden armrests was directly in front of her, facing the right-hand side of the computer closest to her. She went to it and sat down, resting her elbows on the armrests and her forehead in her hands. She closed her eyes, Jonny's words still humming in her ears: "*I can't, Penny. I don't know how.*"

But he *had* to know how! If he could change them into superstars, there *had* to be a way that he could change them back!

She lifted her head and looked at him. His worried blue eyes looked back at her. There couldn't be any delay in trying. Now that she was here with Jonny she was going to *force* him to try. She could see now that he was concerned, frightened.

"Jonny," she said, trying to keep her voice calm, steady, "you've got to do something. You can't say you can't. You've got to change those girls back."

He looked more worried than ever. "Oh, man, Penny. I didn't think . . . I didn't realize what I did. I mean, I never dreamed that Karen — my own *sister* — Shari, and the others would stay that way. I told you, I thought it all would be just temporary."

"But it isn't," Penny said tersely. "Look at Karen. She —" She cut herself off. How could Jonny even try to restore one of the girls to her normal self if none of them was present?

"Where's Karen now?" Penny asked sharply.

Jonny shrugged. "I don't know. Probably at our aunt's. She's been going there a lot lately instead of to her friends'."

"Call her," Penny suggested. "Tell her to come home. Tell her it's important."

Jonny looked at her, fear in his eyes.

"Go on," Penny insisted, looking around and noticing a telephone at the other side of the computer in front of him. "Call her right now. You know your aunt's number?"

He nodded, picked up the phone, dialed, and asked for Karen. A few seconds later he hung up. His eyes sought Penny's. "She's in the pool, and she doesn't want to come out," he said, his velvety voice sounding harsh and hurt now.

Penny stared at him. She thought of Shari, of Faye, of Jean, Jonny's most recent victim. Jean had walked out of Jonny's house less than half an hour ago and had probably gone home. If any of the girls could return, it would be Jean, Penny thought. Excitement sprang up in her as she told Jonny to call her and have her come over immediately.

Jonny looked up Jean's number in the phone book and dialed. Seconds later he hung up. "There's no answer," he said, his face looking as lifeless as his voice sounded.

Penny froze. Oh, no! What now? Should Jonny call Faye, too, and see if she'd come?

Faye was Penny's best friend. That is, she was until Jonny had changed her into a superplayer and left her, as he had left the others, like a robot as far as emotion was concerned. Penny didn't know if they were friends anymore. The part of her that Penny had known so well, that had been active and bubbly and always filled to the brim with fun and laughter, was now dormant. Or maybe dead.

Penny shuddered at the thought and had to say something to drive it out of her mind.

"There's one other thing we can try," she said, the words rushing out of her without her thinking too much about them.

"What?" Jonny asked, curious.

"Put those electrodes on *me*. Change *me*."

Jonny's eyes widened. "Penny! You know what you're saying?"

"Yes!" She was clear-minded now. She knew *exactly* what she was saying. "You run the experiment through several stages, don't you? I mean, you just don't turn the computer on and *puff!* the change has been done?"

"Right. There are five stages," replied Jonny. "Start. Increase power by one. Then by two. Then three, and so on."

Penny's heart pounded as her hope suddenly revived. "Okay. Let's start cracking. Get out those electrodes."

Again Jonny stared at her, as if he were giving her another chance to change her mind. But her stern, demanding look took the place of words. He rolled the chair on its small wheels to the front of the keyboard and monitor beside Penny, pulled out the electrodes, and stuck the suction cups on her wrists, two on each. Then he switched on the computer and waited for it to warm up. In seconds the screen lighted up, and Jonny began to punch some keys. Instantly the date flashed up on the top left corner of the screen, then, underneath it, the time: 4:22 P.M. The monitor was located just back of the keyboard, far enough for Penny to see what was appearing on the screen, even though it was at a difficult angle.

Striking the letters one at a time, Jonny typed "MU-CH-PH." Underneath the capital letters appeared the line "INFORMA-TION RECEIVED. NEXT, PLEASE."

"What does MU-CH-PH mean?" Penny wanted to know.

"Muscular Change Phase," Jonny answered. "Now, don't keep asking me questions. Okay?"

"Okay," Penny replied, reluctant, for she really wanted to know what he did — every step of it — to effect the change. After all, wasn't she volunteering to be his "victim" now? But she let him continue pounding the keyboard without interrupting, and only watched the words as they popped up on the screen. Also, asking Jonny questions every time he pounded out a word might bother him so much he'd make mistakes, thereby delaying their experiment. And they didn't need that.

"MU-CH-PH II" appeared next on the screen, and almost instantly Penny felt a faint prickle shooting through her arms, her stomach, her legs, and her head. It only lasted a second, but the sensation left her staring at the tubes extending to her wrists as if they had suddenly turned into live snakes.

Jonny again struck a few keys, and "WRONG" popped up on the screen. He erased it, struck another series of keys, and this time "OKAY" came up, followed by "PROCESS IN PERFECT COORDINATION. PROCEED WITH CARE. STRIKE THE PROPER CODE WORD EXACTLY EVERY TWENTY SECONDS."

"There!" Penny heard him say, and she

saw a smile of satisfaction come over his face. Obviously he was on the right track now.

But fear suddenly crept into Penny's thoughts. Her idea was to have Jonny change her as he had changed the other girls, and to tell him to stop after having reached one of the higher-powered phases. But she'd been so eager to volunteer for the conversion that she had completely forgotten to tell him!

She had to make sure to tell him to stop while her faculties were still intact. If Jonny went too far, her mind would be affected, she'd forget to yell "Stop," and she would become another super softball athlete! She had to make sure that would not happen! Otherwise, how long would she and the other girls remain in that state? Probably forever — unless someone else tried to help Jonny restore them back to normal. But who knew who that would be? Or when? No. It had to be done now.

Jonny was looking at his digital wristwatch. Suddenly he turned his attention back to the keyboard and began to strike the keys again. "MU-CH-PH III" appeared on the screen. Then, directly beneath it: "OKAY. POWER INCREASED. MUSCLES IN

ARMS AND LEGS GIVEN TEN MICRO-ELECTRIC CHARGES."

There was a slight pause, then new words appeared on the screen: "STOMACH MUSCLES FIRMING. CHEST MUSCLES FIRMING. HOLD FOR TWENTY SEC-ONDS, THEN PRESS NEXT CODE WORD."

Penny felt the same prickling sensation running through her legs, arms, and other parts of her body that she had felt before. But something else was different now. Something about her mind. It seemed to be a little sluggish. It was time. TIME!

Stop! she wanted to yell. Stop!

But the words would not come.

THIRTEEN

PENNY BRACED HERSELF, tightened her fists, and felt her neck muscles firming.

Stop! Stop! her brain screamed.

But no sound came out of her mouth. No sound reached her ears.

She tried again . . . and again. Then, suddenly — like a dam bursting — her voice broke from her throat, her mouth, and echoed in her ears. "STOP! STOP! STOP!"

Quickly, Jonny stopped the power and stared at her. He looked rigid, wide-eyed. "You okay?" he said, worried.

Penny, her eyes closed, shook her head.

She felt exhausted, shaky. "I'm okay," she said, her voice just above a whisper.

"Good. I was worried for a minute." He inhaled deeply, sighed. "Now what? I'm stuck."

Penny opened her eyes, stared at him. She couldn't believe her own thoughts. Had Jonny been so absorbed in the success of his experiment that he hadn't thought about how to change the girls back to their normal selves? Amazing!

"You've got to reverse the procedure!" Penny said, trying hard to think clearly, to keep her wits about her. "Can you do that?"

He looked back at the machine. "I don't know," he said numbly.

"But you've got to try!" Penny cried. "Don't just sit there!"

She had an urge to start pounding the keys herself, but the tubes leading from the computer to her wrists were too short. They would pull off. And they *had* to stay on, otherwise how could she and Jonny know that their attempt to reverse the strength-building procedure was working?

Jonny kept staring at the keys in front of him. He seemed to be in deep concentration. Perspiration beaded his forehead, glistened on his face.

"What are you *waiting* for?" Penny exclaimed after watching him for almost a full minute. She was getting more impatient by the second. Her nerves seemed to be stretched to the breaking point.

"I'm thinking!" Jonny answered, a drop of perspiration falling onto a key.

She looked at him. "Sorry," she said, her voice barely audible.

Finally Jonny struck a key, then another, and another. Penny saw the words "REVERSE PROCEDURE" appear on the screen.

Quickly below it appeared the line: "NOT PROGRAMMED."

Penny felt a cry start in her throat, but she held it in. Of course the reverse procedure wasn't programmed. In that case . . . She looked at Jonny, saw him staring intently at the screen. Was he thinking what *she* was thinking?

He started to pound the keys again. "ELIMINATE MU-CH-PH III. RETURN TO MU-CH-PH II."

"HOLD IT!" The words appeared immediately below the line. "ELIMINATE IS NOT IN OUR STANDARD WORD USAGE. SUBSTITUTE."

"Bull!" Jonny snapped, disgusted.

He punched a key, erasing the word "ELIMINATE," thought a few seconds, and typed "DELETE."

Instantly the line beginning with the words "HOLD IT!" vanished, and the word "OKAY" appeared in its place.

Jonny glanced sideways at Penny and smiled. Penny smiled back. He punched in the words "DELETE MU-CH-PH III. RE-TURN TO MU-CH-PH II."

Almost immediately Penny felt a faint pulsing sensation in her wrists, which shot through her arms, her torso, her legs, and her brain. She closed her eyes, waiting for a reaction to that sensation.

There *was* a difference! A change! But right now, she wouldn't have been able to describe the feeling if she'd had to. She just *knew* that the strength-building procedure *was reversing.*

"Did you feel anything?" Jonny asked.

"Yes!" she whispered, happily. "Drop it down to the next phase."

He struck some keys. Again she felt a pulsing sensation, and a change. It was working. *It was working!*

"How do you feel now?" Jonny asked again.

She opened her eyes and looked at him. She could still feel tingling in her arms, her legs, throughout her body. But not as much as before. "Okay," she said. "Down to the next phase."

Jonny reversed the muscular phase procedure to I. And finally to 0.

"Now how do you feel?" he asked.

Penny sat still a minute, waiting to see if *all* that tingling sensation was gone. If *all* her body muscles felt normal again.

And they did! They did!

"It worked, Jonny! It worked!" she cried, yanking the cups off her wrists herself. Then she jumped off the chair, threw her arms around Jonny, and hugged him fiercely. "I feel exactly like I did before, Jonny! Exactly!"

Happy tears blurred her eyes, and she wiped them away with the palms of her hands. "Now all we have to do is get the girls back here," she said excitedly, "and reverse the procedure on them."

"I just hope that won't be a problem," replied Jonny, the expression on his face a mixture of triumph and worry — triumph over what they had accomplished in being able to restore the girls back to normal again, worry that the girls might not want to sit in front of the computer, put the electrodes on their wrists again, and go through the reversal procedure.

Suddenly there was a sound in another part of the house. The front door had opened and closed. Penny heard footsteps.

"That's Karen!" Jonny whispered.

"Good!" Penny whispered back. "Invite her in here! Explain to her what you must do!"

"Suppose she won't cooperate?"

"She must!" Penny's eyes widened as she looked into Jonny's worried blue eyes. "She must, Jonny! She'll *have* to cooperate!" Karen and the other girls just could not continue to go through life in their present condition.

"Stay here. I'll be right back," said Jonny.

He left the room. A few seconds later Penny heard him talking to his sister. Penny heard Karen answer him, but her voice and Jonny's were so soft that Penny couldn't hear what they said.

Then Penny heard footsteps approaching the room. A moment later Jonny came in, holding onto Karen's hand. At the sight of Penny, Karen's eyes widened, and she stopped.

"Please, Karen," Jonny said, his velvety voice never as tender as it was now. "Please. Penny's here to help me. To help you. I told you that. Now, sit on that chair and I'll put the electrodes back on your wrists like I did before. Only this time you'll become normal again. Do you understand? Normal."

Karen didn't budge, as if she were mulling Jonny's words over and over again in her mind. "*Please,*" Jonny whispered again, so softly that Penny could barely hear him.

Then Karen moved, going to the chair at the side of the computer, sitting down on it, and resting her arms on the chair's armrests. Calmly, Jonny picked up the cups of the electrodes and put them on her wrists. Then he sat down in front of the keyboard and monitor and once again began punching the keys, starting by putting in the date and time, followed by the code words: "MU-CH-PH." He looked at them for a moment, then added the Roman numeral "V." Then "RESPOND, PLEASE."

Instantly, underneath the line he had written, a sentence appeared: "INFORMATION RECEIVED. NEXT, PLEASE."

"Hold your breath," Jonny whispered, as he typed the line "DELETE MU-CH-PH V." A second . . . two seconds passed, as Penny held her breath, waiting to see what the computer was going to say.

The reply came: "OKAY."

"All *right!*" Penny cried spontaneously, throwing her fists into the air. Jonny looked so pleased that Penny thought he was going to let out a happy cry, too. But he restrained himself, glancing across at his sister instead. Penny looked at Karen. The girl's eyes were closed, but Penny noticed a slight movement of her arms and the rest of her body, a reaction to the pulsing sensation she felt coming from the computer through the tubes and into her body.

Twenty seconds later Jonny typed another line: "DELETE MU-CH-PH IV."

"OKAY," responded the computer again on the next line. Once again Penny saw Karen's reaction as the computer reduced the muscular strength in her body and restored her emotional reactions — her *feelings* — closer to normal.

It's working, Penny thought, breathless. *It's really working.*

Twenty seconds later, Jonny pressed the buttons to delete Phase III. Then Phase II. And, finally, Phase I. 0 popped up on the screen.

Silent, tense, Penny watched Karen's face as Jonny shut off the computer and removed the electrodes from his sister's wrists. Karen sat still a moment, staring straight ahead, unmoving — and Penny was seized by the fear that the reversal hadn't fully worked on Karen. Then, suddenly, a broad, bright smile came over Karen's face, and she threw her arms around her brother, hugging him fiercely as tears filled her eyes. Then, still wordless, she turned to Penny and flung her arms around her.

"Penny! Oh, Penny!" she finally cried. "I feel so much better! So much better! Thanks! Thanks trillions!"

Penny felt a lump form in her throat as she returned Karen's squeeze. "I do, too, Karen," she whispered huskily, blinking away the tears that filled her own eyes. "I never felt better in my life."

She closed her eyes tightly to clear them

of tears, then pulled back from Karen and looked at Jonny.

"Now we've got to get the other girls here," she said, relieved, "and get them back to normal."

"Right," replied Jonny, looking fresh and relieved, too, as if a tremendous weight had been lifted from his shoulders. "I'll start calling them right now. The ones we can't get today we'll get tomorrow."

He was already dialing the telephone before the last few words were out of his mouth.

FOURTEEN

THE DAY WAS BLEAK AND DREARY when the Hawks played the Comets on Tuesday afternoon, but there was a sparkle in Penny's eyes as if the sun were really shining. Coach Parker was in the third-base coaching box, and Penny in the first-base coaching box, both clapping and yelling for the Hawks' leadoff hitter to start the game rolling with a hit. The leadoff hitter was Karen Keech.

Maxine Jackson, the tall, wiry girl pitching for the Comets, whipped in the first underhand pitch, and Karen let it go by.

"Steeerike!" yelled the umpire, a big,

112

broad-shouldered man who seemed to be about twice as tall as the Comets catcher.

Karen glanced back at him with a defiant look. Then, as if his size changed her mind about what she was thinking, she turned and faced the pitcher again.

Penny couldn't help but smile. Karen was her old self again, that was for sure. "Drive it, Karen!" Penny yelled. "Start it off, kid!"

Maxine's next pitch was knee high and directly over the plate. Karen swung and topped the ball, hitting a dribbler down to third. The Comets third baseman ran in a few steps, scooped up the easy bouncer, and pegged it to first, beating Karen by two steps. One out.

"That's okay, kid," Penny said, thumping Karen on the back as the girl turned to the right at first base and started to head back toward the Hawks dugout. "Get 'em the next time."

Karen smiled at her. "Right," she said. Even being put out did not keep a sparkle from shining in her eyes, too.

Melanie was up next and singled to right, drawing loud applause from the crowd. She had hit the ball well in the game against the

Hard Hats last week, but each hit had landed in a Hard Hats' glove. "Nice drive, Mel," Penny said.

But it was the next hitter, Shari Chung, that Penny was anxious to see bat. Then Faye. And finally Jean. After each of them had been "deprogrammed," they all had *seemed* to be normal again. They all had *said* they felt their same old selves again. Still, Penny thought that the only place *that* could be proved was on the softball field.

Shari came to the plate, looking excited and eager — almost overeager — to get a hit. But, Penny thought, Shari had *always* looked excited and almost overeager *before*. So, in essence, she *was* the same girl again. The question was, How was her performance going to be at bat?

Shari swung twice, missing the pitch both times, then popped a fly to the shortstop.

A disappointed groan sprang from the Hawks' fans. Even Penny said, "That's okay, Shari. You'll be up again." But there was a smile in Penny's eyes, and joy in her heart. Shari *was* the same girl again in every re-spect.

"Penny! Come in! You follow Faye!" a deep, drawling voice shouted from the bench, and Penny saw Harold Dempsey standing in the dugout.

Penny ran in, and Debbie Brohill ran out to take her place in the coaching box. Penny paused in front of the pile of bats, selected her favorite, then straightened up and looked directly at Harold.

"It's lucky for you, Harold, that Jonny figured out how to change everyone back. That was awful!"

Harold looked at the ground. "I had no idea they'd all start acting that way. It was *weird*. And scary."

"Well, I hope it's all over now. We'll see." Penny looked hard at Harold. She just couldn't figure him out. Then she got into the on-deck circle and watched Faye take a hard cut at a pitch, then crack a single between first and second bases. But the hit was not an *extraordinary* hit, Penny told herself. *Or was it?* Did she have to wait for Faye to bat again before she'd really be sure?

Melanie ran to second base and then to third on the hit. Penny came up next. She felt nervous and worried. She'd been watching Maxine Jackson closely; the pitcher had terrific speed.

Crack! Penny drove the first pitch out to

deep left field for a double, clearing the bases and putting the Hawks on the scoreboard. Her heart pounded joyously as the crowd cheered. "Way to go, Penny!" a fan yelled, and Penny recognized Jonny's voice. She looked for his face in the stands and finally saw it, beaming happily under that thatch of blond hair. She smiled, lifted her hand briefly to wave to him, and he waved back. Her heart raced.

Sophie Kowalski, up next, fouled off three pitches, then struck out. Three outs. Hawks 2, Comets 0.

The Comets scored twice in the bottom of the first inning, however, tying up the game. Then, leading off for the Hawks in the top of the second, Jean Zacks struck out, and now Penny was more certain than ever that at least *three* of the girls — Karen, Shari, and Jean — were back to their normal selves again. There was still a shadow of a doubt about Faye.

The half-inning ended with the Hawks not scoring, leaving three girls stranded on the bases, including Karen, who had drawn a walk.

The Comets went hitless at their turn at

bat. Then Shari led off the top of the third with a fly to the right fielder, and Faye stepped into the box, digging her toes into the dirt, waving the bat in small circles over her right shoulder like a big-leaguer anxious to rap that ball over the fence.

It didn't happen. Faye swung at the first pitch, a perfect down-the-pipe fast ball, and sent it dribbling lazily to the pitcher. Maxine scooped it up and threw Faye out by six feet.

Great! a voice screamed happily inside of Penny as she watched Faye from the on-deck circle. *Faye's okay!* Oh, it would've been much better if Faye had knocked one between the infielders, or had even doubled. The Hawks could use all the hits they could get. But the weak hit was a true sign that Faye wasn't a manufactured super athlete any longer.

When she came running back from first base, Penny said to her, "Tough luck, Faye. Better luck next time."

Faye shrugged and said, "I'll *kill* it the next time."

Penny laughed. Hearing that was all she needed to know that Faye, and all the other girls, were back to their normal, natural selves again.

* * *

The Comets won the game 11 to 9, but Penny — and four other girls, at least — didn't really mind. Winning it or losing it wasn't all that important today. Something else had been more important than ten wins, and it was that something that made the world bright again, and the sun shine again — in spite of the gray clouds.

Penny saw a boy running hard across the field from the grandstand. It was Jonny, his blond hair bouncing, his wide, handsome face shining. Penny's heart pounded. What a change in him, she thought. He looked so much better now that he was relieved of that terrible secret.

"Tough game to lose!" he exclaimed, breathing normally in spite of the sprint from the grandstand. "But" — he shrugged as he met Penny's eyes — "you can't have everything."

"Right," Penny agreed, smiling.

"Excuse me!" a deep, drawling voice cut in.

Penny looked behind her. The stocky, dark-haired scorekeeper entered the circle. "What's on your mind, Harold? A movie next Saturday afternoon?"

Harold stared at her. "No more movies for a while."

His dark, searching eyes rested on her a moment longer, then shifted slowly over the other faces. "Actually, I had a picnic for the team in mind," he said finally. "What do you think? In celebration of our natural athletes."

"Sounds good to me!" Faye piped up, smiling. "You can take Shari and me, Harold. Jonny can take Jean and Penny!"

Harold grinned, his face beaming. He was glad things were back to normal. "Fine with me, Faye," he said. "How about you, Jonny? You for it?"

"One hundred percent," Jonny replied. He took Penny's hand, squeezed it, and Penny squeezed it back.

"Where shall we go?" she asked quietly.

"Who cares?" he said.

How many of these Matt Christopher sports classics have you read?

- ❏ Baseball Pals
- ❏ The Basket Counts
- ❏ Catch That Pass!
- ❏ Catcher with a Glass Arm
- ❏ Challenge at Second Base
- ❏ The Counterfeit Tackle
- ❏ The Diamond Champs
- ❏ Dirt Bike Racer
- ❏ Dirt Bike Runaway
- ❏ Face-Off
- ❏ Football Fugitive
- ❏ The Fox Steals Home
- ❏ The Great Quarterback Switch
- ❏ Hard Drive to Short
- ❏ The Hockey Machine
- ❏ Ice Magic
- ❏ Johnny Long Legs
- ❏ The Kid Who Only Hit Homers
- ❏ Little Lefty
- ❏ Long Shot for Paul
- ❏ Long Stretch at First Base
- ❏ Look Who's Playing First Base
- ❏ Miracle at the Plate
- ❏ No Arm in Left Field
- ❏ Red-Hot Hightops
- ❏ Return of the Home Run Kid
- ❏ Run, Billy, Run
- ❏ Shortstop from Tokyo
- ❏ Soccer Halfback
- ❏ The Submarine Pitch
- ❏ Supercharged Infield
- ❏ Tackle Without a Team
- ❏ Tight End
- ❏ Too Hot to Handle
- ❏ Touchdown for Tommy
- ❏ Tough to Tackle
- ❏ Wingman on Ice
- ❏ The Year Mom Won the Pennant

All available in paperback from Little, Brown and Company

Join the Matt Christopher Fan Club!

To become an official member of the Matt Christopher Fan Club,
send a self-addressed, stamped legal-size envelope to:

Matt Christopher Fan Club
34 Beacon Street
Boston, MA 02108